# Cloud Island

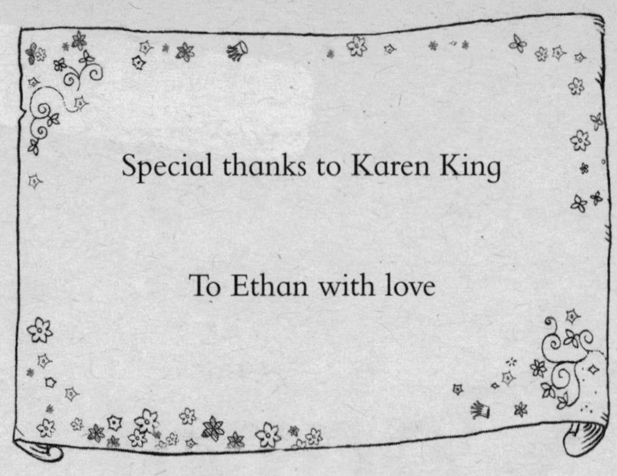




ISBN 978-0-545-53555-7



12 11 10 9 8 7 6 5 4 3 14 15 16 17 18 19/0

Printed in the U.S.A. 40
First Scholastic printing, March 2014

# Cloud Island

ROSIE BANKS

Scholastic Inc.

# Contents


A Message from the Secret Kingdom 1

Up in the Clouds 17

Trouble at the Rainbow Pools 29

Cloudquake 43

A Sweet Solution 53

Storm Sprites Again 69

Rain, Rain, Go Away 81

# A Message from the Secret Kingdom

"I wish we didn't have so much homework to do," sighed Ellie Macdonald as she walked home from school with her friends. "I've got to write a story for English and I don't know where to start!"

"Let's all do our homework together at my house," suggested Jasmine Smith. "We can put some music on and help one another."

"Great idea," agreed Summer Hammond, linking arms with Jasmine and Ellie. "Even homework can be fun when you do it with friends."

"I wouldn't go that far." Ellie grinned, her green eyes twinkling. "But it's better than doing it on your own."

Laughing, they all made their way to Jasmine's house and hurried into the kitchen.

A big bag of chocolate cookies and a note were sitting on the kitchen table. Jasmine picked up the note and read it out loud:

*"'Hi, Jasmine, I'm sure you've brought Ellie and Summer back with you, so share these with them! There's some homemade lemonade in the fridge as well. See you at five. Mom.'"*

"Your mom's so nice!" said Summer.

Jasmine smiled. "I wonder what made her think you'd be with me?"

"Yeah, you would think we spent all our time together," joked Ellie.

Summer giggled. She, Jasmine, and Ellie all lived in a little town called Honeyvale, and went to the same school. They had been best friends since they were little, and they went over to one another's houses so often that they all felt like home!

Jasmine opened the fridge and took out a big jug of lemonade while Summer grabbed three glasses and a plate.

"Now, let's deal with our homework," said Jasmine, putting everything on a tray and leading the way upstairs. "Then we can start having some real fun."

"Hey, you've got the Magic Box on your dressing table!" exclaimed Ellie as they all spilled into Jasmine's bedroom, which was quite small, but beautifully decorated. The walls were a gorgeous hot-pink color, and red floaty netting hung down over the bed.

"I didn't want to miss a message from the Secret Kingdom!" Jasmine said.

They all looked at the beautiful wooden box. It was covered with intricate carvings of fairies and unicorns, and had a mirrored lid studded with six green stones. It looked like a jewelry box, but it was *much* more than that.

"I slept with it under my pillow last time I was taking care of it!" Ellie laughed.

The girls had found the Magic Box at a school rummage sale, when it had mysteriously appeared in front of them. It belonged to King Merry, the ruler of the Secret Kingdom.

The Secret Kingdom was a magical world that no one knew existed — no one except Jasmine, Summer, and Ellie! It was a beautiful crescent moon-shaped island, where mermaids, unicorns, pixies, and elves all lived happily together.

But the kingdom was in terrible trouble. Queen Malice, the king's horrible sister, was so angry that the people of the Secret Kingdom had chosen King Merry to be their ruler instead of her that she had sent six horrible thunderbolts into the kingdom to cause all kinds of trouble. Summer, Jasmine, and Ellie had already found two of the thunderbolts and broken their nasty spells.

"I wish we could go on another magical adventure," sighed Ellie.

"Me too," agreed Jasmine, taking her books out of her backpack and sprawling out on the carpet. She tucked her long dark hair behind her ears. "Come on, let's get this over with," she said, reaching for a chocolate cookie.

Ellie got out her English book and

started chewing on her pencil. She was looking around the room, trying to come up with an idea for her story, when something caught her eye. "I don't think we'll be doing homework after all!" she cried in delight. "The Magic Box is glowing!"

The girls all jumped up to look. They crowded around the box, watching excitedly as, letter by letter, words started to form in the magic mirror.

"I wonder what mischief Queen Malice is up to now," said Jasmine, shuddering at the thought of the horrid queen and her wicked plans to make everyone in the kingdom as miserable as she was.

"We'll have to solve the riddle to find out," said Summer as she studied the words in the mirror. Then she slowly read them out loud:

*"'A thunderbolt there will be found*
*Way up high above the ground.*
*A white and fluffy floating land*
*Needs you all to lend a hand!'"*

Jasmine quickly wrote the riddle down before the words disappeared into the mirror. "What does it mean?" she asked.

Ellie looked puzzled. "A floating land — it must be an island."

"Let's check the map," said Jasmine. "We might be able to spot it."

As if it had heard them, the Magic Box opened up, revealing the six compartments inside. Only two of the spaces were filled, one by a map of the Secret Kingdom that King Merry had given them after their first visit, and the other by a little silver unicorn horn. It was small, but it had enormous power — whoever held it could talk to animals!

Summer carefully took out the map and spread it out gently on Jasmine's floor. The three girls sat around it, their heads touching as they peered at it excitedly. There were a few small islands in Mermaid Reef, and a couple more off the shore of Glitter

Beach. They all moved magically on the map as the aquamarine sea bobbed up and down, but none of them looked white or fluffy.

"It's not here!" Summer said anxiously.

"But it has to be!" cried Ellie. "We have to solve the riddle so we can get to the Secret Kingdom and find the thunderbolt before something horrible happens!"

Jasmine stood and started pacing up and down the middle of her room with a worried expression on her face.

"Let's read the riddle again," Summer suggested. "We must be missing something. 'A white and fluffy floating land.' Well, these islands aren't white or fluffy."

" 'Way up high above the ground . . .' " Jasmine muttered to herself. Then she glanced down at the map and laughed.

Summer and Ellie were still searching the bottom of the map, looking at every inch of sea. But Jasmine had realized something. "We shouldn't be looking in the sea!" she cried. "We should be looking in the sky!"

"Of course!" said Ellie with a grin. "What's white and fluffy and floats?"

"A cloud!" exclaimed Summer.

"And here's Cloud Island!" Ellie exclaimed, pointing to a puffy white cloud at the top of the map. "That must be it. Let's summon Trixi!"

The girls put their hands on the Magic Box, pressing their fingers against the pretty green stones on its carved wooden lid.

"The answer is Cloud Island," Jasmine whispered.

Suddenly there was a flash of light, followed by a squeal. Trixibelle had appeared, but the little pixie was trapped in the netting over Jasmine's bed!

"Keep still!" Jasmine cried as the pixie twisted around. She was trying to free herself, but was only getting more and more caught up.

"I'm trying!" Trixi cried, giving a yelp as she tumbled off her leaf.

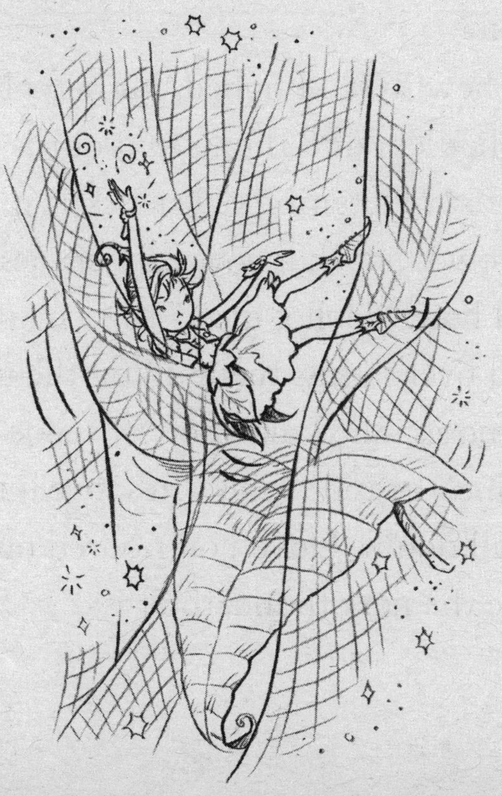

Ellie, Jasmine, and Summer quickly climbed up onto Jasmine's bed to untangle Trixi from the mesh. Ellie's nimble fingers carefully unwrapped the netting from Trixi's flower hat, while Jasmine and Summer helped Trixi pull her arms and legs free.

"There!" Ellie said as she untangled the last bit.

"Whew!" Trixi sighed, jumping back onto her leaf and flying in a quick twirl before straightening out her skirt and the flower hat that covered her messy blond hair. "Hello, girls," she exclaimed, flying over to kiss them all on the tips of their noses. She landed on the edge of Jasmine's bedside table. "It's lovely to see you all again. Have you figured out where the next thunderbolt is?"

"We think it's somewhere called Cloud Island," Summer said.

Trixi nodded. "There's no time to waste! We need to go to the kingdom right away."

The girls all looked excitedly at one another. They were off on another magical adventure — this time to an island in the sky!

# Up in the Clouds

As the girls watched, Trixi tapped the Magic Box with her ring and chanted a spell:

*"The evil Queen has trouble planned.*
*Brave helpers fly to save our land."*

Her words appeared on the mirrored lid and then soared toward the ceiling, separated into sparkles, and tumbled down again in a colorful burst, whizzing around the girls' heads until they formed a whirlwind. The rushing air picked the girls up, and moments later Ellie, Summer, and Jasmine were dropped onto something springy. It was the softest landing ever!

Summer looked around in astonishment. It felt like she was on a huge bouncy bed, but all she could see around her was white. Hesitantly, she put out her hand to touch the fluffy stuff, and then grinned as she realized — she was standing on a cloud!

Summer jumped with glee. As she bounced higher and higher, she could see the clouds laid out below her like giant stepping stones. Beneath that she could see the aquamarine sea and the crescent moon-shaped island of the Secret Kingdom!

Summer looked down as she heard a noise from the cloud just below her. It was Jasmine, bouncing up and down so excitedly that her tiara fell off.

"Whoops!" laughed Jasmine, catching it. "We can't lose these."

"Definitely not!" Summer agreed.

The beautiful tiaras magically appeared on their heads every time they visited the Secret Kingdom, and they showed everyone in the land that Jasmine, Summer, and Ellie were Very Important Friends of King Merry!

Summer pressed her tiara firmly onto her head, and then looked around for Ellie. She soon caught a glimpse of red hair on a cloud below Jasmine's. Ellie was lying flat on the cloud, holding on to the surface as tightly as she could!

"Oh dear!" Summer cried. "Ellie's scared of heights, and we are very high. How do we get down to her?"

"We bounce, of course!" Jasmine replied,

fearlessly leaping down to a nearby cloud, and then jumping straight down to Ellie's. "Wheeeeeee!"

Summer took a deep breath and followed her. She flew through the air and landed next to Ellie on the soft cloud.

Ellie groaned as the cloud shook. "Why do we always arrive so high up?"

"Don't worry!" said Trixi, flying down next to them. "You can't fall. These are trampoline clouds! They're made so that you can get from one cloud to the next. If you do a little jump, they'll spring you right over to the next cloud. They're really bouncy — just like trampolines!"

"Trampoline clouds are amazing!" Jasmine said, bouncing high and doing a somersault. "Come on, Ellie. Try bouncing!"

Summer helped Ellie stand up, and she and Jasmine both held on to their friend's hands as she started jumping. Soon Ellie was having so much fun she almost forgot how high up they were!

"Cloud Island is down there," Trixi said, pointing at a cloud far down below.

The girls all peered over the edge. Cloud Island was much bigger than the little trampoline clouds that led down to it. It seemed to be about the size of Honeyvale, and there were funny little houses perched on the cloud.

"Race you down there!" Jasmine called, and before the others could stop her, she had leapt to the next cloud.

"It's easy!" she laughed as Ellie looked at her anxiously.

"I'll hold your hand," Summer said kindly. Ellie closed her eyes and gripped Summer's hand tightly. They jumped on the spot and then leapt onto the next cloud down. It *was* easy — and it was so much fun!

They went from one trampoline cloud to another, passing lots of surprised-looking birds along the way. The birds were flying from cloud to cloud with envelopes in their beaks.

"Those are messenger doves," Trixi explained. "They bring notes up to the clouds from the kingdom."

Soon Cloud Island was only a few jumps away.

"Hey, look at those meadows!" called Jasmine. On top of the cloud were fields of pale yellow fluffy flowers!

"They look like dandelions . . . no, like cotton balls!" exclaimed Ellie.

"And they're exactly the same color as fluffy yellow ducklings!" Summer giggled.

"They're fluff flowers," Trixi told her. "The weather imps grow them to make clouds. But they also make a wonderful landing place," she added, flying into the flowers and scattering fluff everywhere!

Jasmine, Ellie, and Summer looked at one another with a grin.

"Three," Jasmine started.

"Two," Summer continued.

"One!" Ellie shrieked.

"Jump!" they all yelled, holding hands as they leapt off the last trampoline cloud and landed on Cloud Island!

The girls lay in the fluff flower field until they'd gotten their breath back. "This is much better than homework!" Ellie giggled, putting fluff in Jasmine's hair. Jasmine laughed and threw some of the silky stuff back at her.

"Don't forget about Queen Malice's thunderbolt," Summer reminded them. "We've got to stop it before it does something horrible to Cloud Island."

Suddenly feeling serious again, the girls brushed themselves off and walked to the edge of the field. In front of them they could see a group of funny little houses and factories and a tall brick chimney with pretty white clouds puffing out of it.

"The fluff flowers are cooked in the cloud factory ovens until they're lighter than air," explained Trixi. "Then they come out of the chimney as clouds." She pointed at a puff of air rising out of the chimney. "Look, there's one that's just been made."

Ellie, Summer, and Jasmine watched in wonder as a fluffy cloud squeezed out of the chimney and floated up into the sky.

"That's the most amazing thing I've ever seen!" gasped Jasmine.

Just then peals of laughter filled the air. The girls turned to see some creatures flying out of the cloud factory on top of mini storm clouds. They had spiky hair, twiggy fingers, and pointy faces.

"Oh no!" Ellie cried. "Storm Sprites!"

# Trouble at the Rainbow Pools

All three girls shuddered as they watched the Storm Sprites zoom out of the cloud factory. The sprites were Queen Malice's horrible helpers, and they made mischief wherever they went!

"They must be here to cause problems," Jasmine whispered to the others.

"What are we going to do?" Summer asked, her face pale.

"Go away!" Ellie yelled as the Storm Sprites hovered overhead, laughing.

"Look, it's those smelly human girls," one of the sprites said, pointing a spiky finger at them.

"Yes, and we're going to stop whatever trouble you've got planned!" Ellie told him, putting her hands on her hips.

"Not this time," another sprite cackled. "This thunderbolt is so well hidden that you'll never find it!"

With a screech of laughter, the Storm Sprites dived toward the girls. Ellie ducked, but Summer and Jasmine didn't move quickly enough. One of the sprites pushed Jasmine as he flew by, and she landed on the cloud with a thud. Another sprite grabbed Summer's tiara and tried to pull it off her head.

"Ouch!" Summer cried out, grabbing hold of her tiara before the sprite could steal it.

"Leave her alone!" came a shout from behind them. A thin girl wearing a fluffy dress was running over, waving her arms at the Storm Sprites. The sprite let go of Summer's tiara and flew up to join the others.

"See you soon!" he said, giggling nastily as they all flew away.

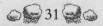

"Are you okay?" asked the girl as she helped Summer up. She had a pretty, smiling face and was wearing an apron that was covered with bits of fluff flowers. "Those Storm Sprites are awful. They're always here stealing our cotton candy."

"Hello there!" Trixi cried in delight, flying over to them. "This is Lolo," Trixi told Ellie, Summer, and Jasmine. "She's a weather imp. Weather imps live on Cloud Island and look after the Secret Kingdom's weather." She turned to Lolo. "This is Ellie, Summer, and Jasmine," she continued, pointing to each girl in turn. "They're our human friends from the Other Realm."

"Thank you for chasing the Storm Sprites away," Summer said, hugging Lolo, who was as tall as she was.

"You're welcome," Lolo said. "It's lovely to meet you. Everyone in the kingdom has been talking about how you saved King

Merry's birthday party and the Golden Games." She looked at them, a concerned expression crossing her face. "But what were the Storm Sprites saying? There isn't a thunderbolt on Cloud Island, is there?"

"We think there might be," said Jasmine.

Lolo's big eyes filled up with tears.

"Don't worry," Summer reassured her. "We'll break Malice's spell and make sure Cloud Island is all right. But we need to find the thunderbolt — the sprites said that it was really well hidden."

"Well, I know every bit of Cloud Island," Lolo told them. "I'll show you around — I'm sure we'll find it!"

Lolo led the girls into the cloud factory to see if they could spot the thunderbolt. Nearly the whole room was taken up with a huge oven, and teams of weather imps were shoveling fluff flowers into it.

"That's the chimney the finished clouds come out of," Lolo explained, pointing to the big pipe coming out of the oven.

The girls looked all around the factory, but there was no sign of the thunderbolt anywhere.

"At least we know what the Storm Sprites were up to," Lolo said, holding up an empty basket. "They've eaten all the cotton candy that was going to be lunch!"

The weather imps looked cranky, but Lolo soon cheered them up. "We'll pick some more," she told them. "We need to check that the thunderbolt isn't in one of the meadows, anyway."

Lolo led Trixi, Summer, Ellie, and Jasmine along to the fluff flower and cotton candy meadows. The girls were delighted to see tiny white cloud bunnies hopping about the fields, chewing on the fluff flower leaves.

"They're so sweet!" Summer squealed as she picked one up and gently stroked its soft fur. It looked just like a real rabbit, but it was much softer and fluffier, and it was as light as a feather. The little bunny looked up at her with deep chocolate-brown eyes, and its little pink nose twitched. "I guess

even our Other Realm bunnies have tails that look like clouds," she said thoughtfully.

"Oooh, cotton candy!" Jasmine said, looking at the meadow of light-pink sugar bushes that stretched out in front of them. "Yum!"

"Try some!" Lolo laughed. "We need to pick some for the cloud factory imps' lunch anyway, thanks to those horrid sprites."

Jasmine reached down and picked a handful. "Cotton candy is my absolute favorite thing!" she squealed, popping it in her mouth. It was so soft it melted on her tongue. "And this is the best cotton candy ever!"

The girls got to work filling up baskets of cotton candy for the cloud factory imps, munching as they went. Soon the baskets were full — and so was Jasmine!

"I think I've eaten too much!" she groaned, feeding the rest of her handful to Summer's bunny.

"I think I'll call him Cotton!" Summer giggled. Cotton hopped after the girls as they took the cotton candy to the cloud factory. He wiggled his nose at them as they went inside, almost as if he was saying good-bye, and then hopped off toward a nearby field.

The weather imps looked after all the weather in the kingdom, so, as well as the cloud factory, there were factories that created raindrops, sunbeams, fog, and snow.

Lolo took Ellie, Jasmine, Summer, and Trixi into the raindrop workshop, where the weather imps made perfect raindrops by dribbling water into drops that were just the right size. Strung along the top of the room were long clotheslines with little gray clouds pinned on them.

"We dry out old rain clouds and recycle them into soft and fluffy clouds," Lolo explained.

As the rain clouds dried out, water dropped down on the imps and the girls below. Trixi, Ellie, Summer, and Jasmine were getting very wet, although the drops were lovely and warm.

"It doesn't normally rain inside!" Ellie joked.

Trixi laughed. "Anything's possible in the Secret Kingdom!"

"I know something you might like," Lolo told the girls. "It has to do with rain — but it's not so wet!"

Lolo led them out of the raindrop workshop and around to some big circles on the ground. Ellie and the others rushed over and gasped — each one was a pool of brilliant, vibrant color.

"Wow!" Ellie said, gazing at the colors. "I've never seen these shades before!"

"These are the rainbow pools," Lolo explained. "We use them to create rainbows in the sky."

Ellie looked at the magical colors in wonder. "I wish my paints were as beautiful as this!" she breathed.

The girls wandered around, looking at the gorgeous pools. Summer couldn't decide which one she liked best! There were ruby reds and dazzling silver-blues, and all different shades of pink. They were all stunning — apart from one that was a purple color, speckled with funny gray bits. "It's a shame this one's got dirt in it," she said sadly.

Lolo rushed over to look. "There's something in here spoiling the color!"

she exclaimed. She plunged her arm into the pool and pulled out a tiny violet plug. There was a loud sucking noise, and the color started swirling around and around, disappearing down the drain.

As the color drained away, the girls could see something black and jagged stuck in the bottom of the pool.

It was Queen Malice's thunderbolt!

# Cloudquake

"Don't worry," said Jasmine, putting her arm around Lolo, who was looking at the rainbow pool sadly. "We'll find a way to get rid of Queen Malice's evil thunderbolt."

But just as she spoke, the cloud beneath their feet started to tremble and shake! Then a thick crack appeared in the cloud, right in front of the violet pool. Ellie,

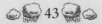

Summer, and Jasmine watched in horror as the crack widened and spread.

Trixi flew her leaf up into the air and looked from side to side. There was a huge jagged split running through the cotton candy fields, past the rainbow pools, all the way up to the sunbeam factory. "It stretches right across the whole island!" she called.

"Aah!" Ellie cried as the cloud shook again. She grabbed on to Jasmine and Summer's hands, and they held one another tightly as the crack in front of them grew wider. Now they could see right through it, down to the kingdom far below.

"The island's breaking in half!" Trixi called from above.

"Oh my goodness!" Lolo gasped. "I've never known a cloudquake as bad as this!"

There was another big tremble, and the crack widened, splitting the island in two. To everyone's horror, the two sides of the island began drifting apart!

The girls looked around in alarm. On their side of the crack were the fluff flower fields and the raindrop workshop, and on the other side, with Lolo and some of the other imps, were the cloud factory and the rainbow pools. Already the gap was too wide to jump across, and the other side of the island was moving farther and farther away from them.

Summer gasped — there, sitting at the edge of the other part of the island, was her cloud bunny, his ears drooping sadly. He was looking over at the fluff flowers, where all the rest of the bunnies were hopping about nervously. "I hope he doesn't try to jump back to his friends," she said anxiously.

"Lolo! Can you look after Cotton?" she called over to the other cloud.

"Of course!" Lolo shouted back. She scooped up the little rabbit and put him in her apron pocket.

"Don't worry," Trixi called as she came flying down next to them. "I'll use my magic to put the island back together again."

She flew over the gap, tapped her ring, and chanted:

*"With this magic, my wish is plain,*
*Cloud Island become one again."*

Showers of purple glitter shot out of her ring and shimmered through the air between the two halves of the island. But nothing happened.

"If Trixi's spell isn't working, this has got to be because of Queen Malice's horrid thunderbolt," Ellie said sadly.

When the weather imps saw that Trixi couldn't fix the island, they started running about frantically.

"What are we going to do?" one shouted. "If the fluff flowers are on one cloud and the cloud factory is on the other, we won't be able to make any new clouds!"

"And without clouds there won't be any rain, and all the flowers and plants in the kingdom will die!" another cried.

"Please don't worry!" Summer called. "This is because of Queen Malice's nasty thunderbolt. But we'll find a way to break its spell and put the island back together again."

"Yes, we'll think of something,"

promised Ellie. "We won't let her get away with it."

"What can we do, though?" Jasmine whispered.

Just then, one of the messenger doves the girls had seen before flew down toward them with an envelope in its beak.

The dove flapped across the gap to Trixi. The little pixie took the note and unfolded it. To the girls' surprise, on it was a tiny moving image of King Merry!

"It's just like the magical map!" Ellie cried.

The king seemed worried, and more messy than normal. His crown looked like it was about to fall off his white curly hair, and his half-moon glasses were lopsided on his nose.

"Is everything all right up there, Trixi?" the king asked, his voice sounding tiny and squeaky. "We just heard an awful cloudquake!"

"We think it's the work of one of Queen Malice's thunderbolts, Sire," Trixi told him sadly. "It's split Cloud Island in half!"

"Oh dear, oh dear." King Merry sounded very upset. "I'll come up there right away and see what I can do to help. I can use the transporter that I've just invented."

Trixi frowned nervously. "Your Majesty —" she started saying. But it was too late. King Merry's face vanished from the paper before she had a chance to finish.

"Oh no," she groaned. "I wish he'd let me magic him here! He invented a transporter last week and it keeps going wrong. Yesterday he tried to transport himself into his bath and he ended up in the sea!"

Suddenly, there was a bright flash and King Merry appeared — right on the edge of the cloud!

"Aah!" he cried, swinging his arms around to balance himself.

The girls ran toward him, but it was too late. With a cry of surprise, King Merry fell over the side!

# A Sweet Solution

"Don't worry — I'll save him!" Trixi called, tapping her ring. The girls rushed to the edge and peered over, but they couldn't see King Merry anywhere.

"Do you think he's okay?" Summer asked anxiously.

Suddenly, there was a very familiar voice from high above them. "Oh gracious me!"

Everyone looked up to see King Merry floating overhead, hanging on to an enormous bunch of brightly colored balloons!

"King Merry!" the girls cried with relief.

"Let them go, King Merry," Trixi called up. "One at a time!" she added — but it was too late. King Merry let go of all the balloons at once and landed on his bottom with a thud, making the cloud wobble.

"It's another cloudquake!" a scared imp shouted.

"Shhh, it's just King Merry," said another.

"Gosh, thank you, Trixibelle," King Merry said as the girls rushed over to help him up. "I don't know what I'd do without you!"

When King Merry got his breath back, Jasmine explained what had been going on.

"This is terrible, just terrible," King Merry declared. "How can Malice do such a horrible thing? We have to stop her!"

Summer twirled her long blond braids thoughtfully. "In Unicorn Valley, the thunderbolt shattered when we undid all the trouble it had caused."

"So if we put the island back together again it might break Queen Malice's spell!" Jasmine agreed.

King Merry took off his crown and scratched his head. He peered at the big gap between the two parts of the island, shaking his head as if he could hardly believe his eyes. "But how can we do that?" he muttered to himself. "Can we stitch it together? No, no. We could glue it together . . ."

"That's it!" Summer cried. "We can glue it with new clouds from the cloud factory!"

"Lolo," she called to the imp on the other cloud. "Can we stick the island back together with new clouds?"

Lolo shook her head. "We can't make clouds quickly enough to repair a crack this big," she replied.

"If only we could stick it together with something else, just while the clouds are being made," Jasmine sighed.

"Maybe we can," Ellie said, thinking. "I've got it!" she said, her eyes gleaming.

"We can glue it back together with cotton candy. It's light and fluffy, like a cloud!"

"And sticky, too!" said Summer.

"That's a brilliant idea," agreed Jasmine.

"Do you think it would work, Trixi?" Summer asked the little pixie. "Is cotton candy sticky enough to mend the island?"

"It should hold the island together long enough for the weather imps to make enough clouds to fix it properly," Trixi replied. "And I can cast an extra-sticky spell to make sure. But I don't know how we can move the other half of the island closer so we can stick it together. I can't use my magic to move it."

"There must be some way we can pull the broken part back over here . . ." muttered Jasmine.

Ellie looked around Cloud Island for

inspiration. Then her eyes rested on the little dove, still perched next to Summer. "The messenger doves!" she cried. "They could flap their wings and blow the broken half back over to us!" She sighed. "If only we could talk to them and explain what we wanted them to do."

With a shimmer, the Magic Box appeared in front of them.

"Of course!" Summer said. "We can use the unicorn horn to talk to them!" Her face broke into a wide grin as she picked up the magical horn the unicorns had given them. It was so tiny — only the size of her little finger — but it gave them a great power. When they held it they had the ability to talk to all the animals in the Secret Kingdom! Summer had often wished that she could understand what her animal friends were saying, and now she'd finally get the chance. She turned to the white dove excitedly and picked up the unicorn horn. "Please, can you help us?" she asked.

Ellie and Jasmine looked at each other in surprise — it sounded to them as if Summer was cooing like a dove!

"Me?" Summer heard the dove coo in a surprised voice. "Why, yes, if I can. What's wrong?"

"He understood me!" Summer gasped in delight. "I can talk to him!

"A cloudquake has split Cloud Island in two," she told the bird. "We were hoping you and your friends could help us put it back together."

The dove looked over at the other side of the island. "What do you want us to do?" he asked.

"Could you gather all of your friends and beat your wings at the same time to make some wind?" Summer asked the dove. "It might be strong enough to blow the broken part back over to us, and then we could stick the island back together again."

"We're going to need a lot of wing power," the dove replied, flapping into the air. "I'll gather the flock."

"He's going to get the others!" Summer told Ellie and Jasmine.

"Thank you!" Ellie and Jasmine shouted and Summer cooed, as the dove flew away.

"This might just work!" Jasmine said, excitedly. "Let's tell Lolo." They hurried to the edge. The other half of the island was farther away than ever, but Lolo was still close enough to hear as the girls shouted the plan over.

"How clever!" Lolo called back. "We'll start making as much cloud as we can, and I'll organize the cotton candy collection on this side."

"And I'll supervise over here!" yelled King Merry. "I love cotton candy . . . I mean, I love gathering cotton candy!"

Trixi smiled, "He'll probably eat more than he collects!" she whispered with a giggle.

The girls, King Merry, and the weather imps all bustled around the cotton candy meadow collecting armfuls of the sticky pink stuff, which they piled up along the edge of the cloud. Even though King Merry and Jasmine couldn't resist nibbling on the delicious cotton candy as they collected it, they still managed to gather more than enough to fix the island.

Trixi flew over the cotton candy heap and recited a spell to make it extra-sticky, then she flew over to the other part of the island to do the same there. Everyone knelt

down and started to spread the pink fluff on the edges of the crack.

"It's a shame the cotton candy isn't white," said Jasmine as she stuck some on. "I hope the pink doesn't show too badly."

"It doesn't matter," Trixi reminded her. "It's only temporary. It just needs to hold together long enough for the weather imps to make more cloud."

"And when we break Queen Malice's thunderbolt, everything will go back to normal anyway!" Summer said cheerfully.

It took a while, but soon their side of the island was covered in the sticky pink stuff.

"Finished!" Ellie cried.

"Just in time!" gasped Jasmine as the flock flew toward them. "Look how many doves there are!"

"Are you ready over there?" Ellie shouted to the other side, but Lolo and the other imps were now too far away to hear.

Trixi flew over to them and came back a few minutes later. "They're ready!" she said.

"Hello, doves!" Summer cooed, holding tightly to the horn. "Can you please start beating your wings to push the two island halves together?"

The little birds circled the broken half of the island and started beating their wings really fast. Their wings made a strong wind, and the broken section gradually started to move. . . .

"It's working!" shouted Ellie shouted, jumping up and down with excitement. "We're getting closer!"

The weather imps gathered on both edges, cheering loudly.

"Well done!" they called to the doves. "Keep going!"

Up and down, up and down, the doves flapped their wings as fast as they could.

"Hoorah! You're nearly there!" shouted King Merry.

Everyone called and waved as the doves pushed the pieces closer and closer together.

But just as the two halves of the island were almost touching, something plummeted from the sky. Four spiky-haired creatures with batlike wings zoomed into the gap and interrupted the cheers with loud shrieks and jeers.

"Aha!" one cried. "The Storm Sprites are here to spoil your day!"

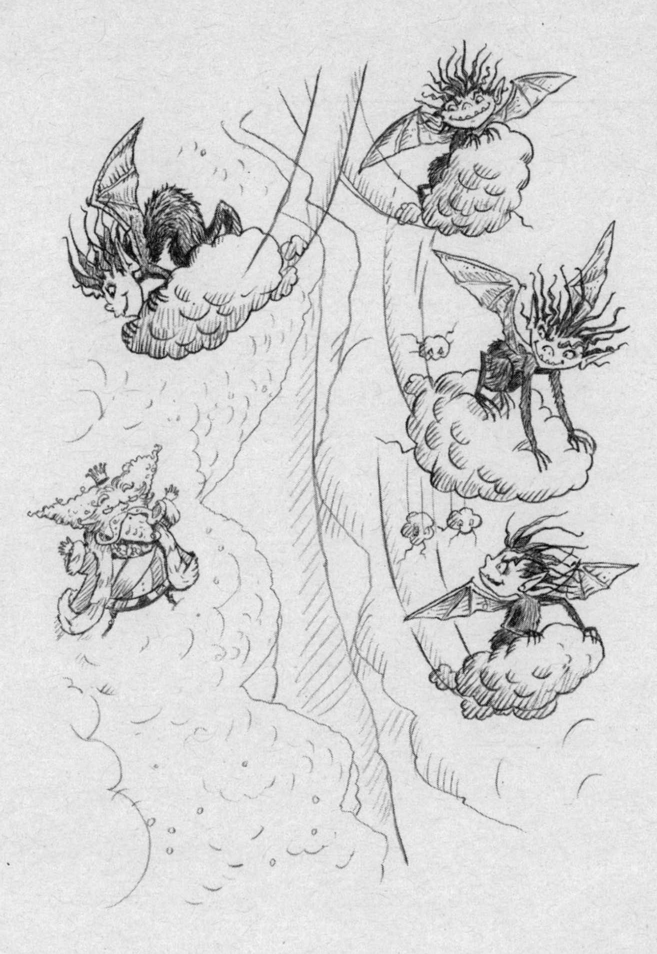

# Storm Sprites Again

The Storm Sprites hovered their storm clouds in the crack, laughing nastily.

"Oh no!" shouted Ellie. "They've come back to stop us from fixing Cloud Island."

"They're so horrible," groaned Summer.

Whooping and cackling, the sprites started beating their powerful batlike wings. The blast of wind almost blew the girls off their feet.

"They're pushing the island apart again!" cried Ellie.

The doves were fighting against the wind as well, and had to perch on the clouds so that they weren't blown away.

"We've got to do something," said Jasmine, looking at the wide gulf of blue sky between the two halves of the island.

"I've got an idea," said Summer. She rushed over to the raindrop workshop and scooped up some of the cotton candy from the heap. "Yum!" she cried loudly. "This cotton candy looks really delicious! Do you want some, Ellie?"

"I don't think we have time. . . ." Ellie stopped as Summer nodded her head over to the Storm Sprites, who had stopped flapping and were looking hungrily at the big pile of cotton candy.

"Oh, thanks, Summer!" she said loudly, taking a bite. "Mmmmm, this is tasty cotton candy. Jasmine, come and have some!"

The Storm Sprites were licking their lips now. One tugged on another's wing. "They've got cotton candy," he said longingly. "Queen Malice never lets us eat cotton candy!"

"Good idea, Summer!" Ellie whispered.

"Food always distracts my brothers, too!" Summer giggled.

"We'll just leave this big pile of delicious cotton candy here while we go over there," Jasmine said, winking at Ellie and Summer.

The three girls walked away, and Ellie peeked over her shoulder. The sprites had all rushed over to the cotton candy and were stuffing it into their mouths.

While they were busy eating, Summer spoke to the doves using the unicorn horn. "Quick! Start blowing the island back together again!" she cooed.

The doves circled the broken piece and beat their wings with all their might. Slowly it started to drift back toward the rest of Cloud Island.

"They've almost got it," whispered Jasmine.

But then the head Storm Sprite turned around. "We've been tricked!" he screeched. "We can't let them fix the island!" he shouted to the other sprites. "We'll be in big trouble if those girls best us again. The queen will lock us in the dungeons!"

The sprites rushed toward the gap, but Ellie, Summer, and Jasmine were quicker. The girls grabbed handfuls of cotton candy and started throwing it at the sprites!

"Take that!" Ellie yelled, throwing a sticky missile at one of the sprites. The candy hit him with a squelchy thud.

"Yuck!" he complained.

The girls took no notice. "Serves you right for being so horrible!" Summer yelled, throwing more cotton candy.

"I'm covered in pink stuff," one sprite whined.

"So am I!" shrieked another.

They tried to pull the cotton candy off one another, but then their hands started sticking together!

The girls, King Merry, Trixi, and the weather imps all giggled at the sticky sprites. They looked so funny covered in pink goo!

"Flap your wings!" the sprite leader shouted to the others from his cloud.

The sprites tried to make some wind to blow the pieces of the island apart, but their wings were so covered with cotton candy that they stuck together and wouldn't flap.

"Retreat!" shouted the leader.

The Storm Sprites jumped on their clouds and zoomed down to the kingdom below.

"We did it!" Ellie cried. The three girls hugged one another in delight. Now that the Storm Sprites were out of the way, the doves were able to blow the broken pieces of the island together. With a jolt, Cloud Island was finally joined up again, the sticky cotton candy holding it fast.

"Hooray!" the imps all cheered, clapping.

Ellie and Jasmine waved. "Thank you!" they called to the doves.

"Thank you so much for helping us," Summer cooed to her dove friend.

"My pleasure," cooed the dove. Then he waved his wings and flew off with the others.

Lolo and the other imps rushed over. Lolo handed the cloud bunny to Summer, and he snuggled up to her again gladly.

"I'm glad you're safe, Cotton," Summer told him as she stroked his fluffy ears. She put him down and he hopped happily back to his bunny friends. One of them jumped toward him and they rubbed noses.

"Now to mend this crack once and for all," Lolo said firmly. "Quick — start making as much cloud as you can," she told the other weather imps.

The imps rushed about, busily collecting fluff flowers and feeding them into the cloud factory.

Summer had an armful of fluff flowers and was bending over to pick more when a dark shadow fell across the ground. She looked up and gasped.

There was a thundercloud heading right for them . . . and on top of it stood a figure who looked horribly familiar!

A tall, thin woman with wild, frizzy hair was leaning over the edge of the cloud. She was wearing a black cloak and a spiky silver crown, and she held a long, sharp staff in her hand.

"It's Queen Malice!" Summer cried.

# Rain, Rain, Go Away

Queen Malice's cloud floated over them and the girls raced after it. It stopped right over the line of cotton candy and a shower of rain began to gush from it.

"Oh no!" gasped Summer as a trickle of pink water oozed out of the crack. "She's trying to wash the cotton candy away! It needs to be sticky, not soggy!"

"So you girls have found another one of my thunderbolts," Queen Malice called down from her thundercloud. "Well, you won't destroy this one! I will break Cloud Island apart and the Secret Kingdom will turn into a dry desert. My useless brother won't know what to do and then you'll all be *begging* me to rule!"

"That won't happen!" Jasmine called back, looking at Queen Malice fiercely as the rain poured down on her. "We won't let you get away with it!"

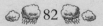

"Silly girl!" Queen Malice cackled. "I'm far more powerful than you. I'm going to destroy Cloud Island, and there's nothing you can do about it!"

There was a fierce crack of lightning and a loud rumble of thunder, and even more rain poured onto the pink cotton candy that was holding the two parts of the cloud together.

"We've got to do something!" cried Ellie.

Queen Malice laughed as everyone on Cloud Island ran about frantically.

Jasmine looked around desperately. "We need to stop the water from falling," she told the others. "Trixi, can you magic something up to catch it? An umbrella or a blanket or something?"

Trixi pointed her ring and suddenly a stripy bucket floated down from the sky.

Jasmine jumped up to catch it, and rushed to put it under the raincloud. More and more buckets appeared, and Ellie, King Merry, Summer, and Lolo all rushed to put them on the crack to protect it from the falling rain. Soon there were hundreds of buckets of all sizes and colors keeping the cotton candy nice and dry. Raindrops plopped noisily into them and the buckets started filling up.

"We need somewhere to empty them out," said Summer, pointing at a small bucket next to her that was almost completely full.

Ellie was standing closest to the edge of Cloud Island. She peered over and saw a pretty forest of tall flowers below. The Storm Sprites were sitting in the center of one of the gigantic flowers, picking cotton candy off of their wings and squabbling loudly.

"Those giant flowers look like they could use a drink," Ellie said.

"And the Storm Sprites could use a bath!" Summer giggled.

As the buckets filled up, Summer, Ellie, Jasmine, King Merry, and all the weather imps started emptying them over the side.

"What are you doing down there?" Queen Malice called, leaning farther over the edge of her cloud to watch them struggling to empty out all the buckets. As soon as they poured one out they had

to come back and take another full bucket. The buckets were filling up faster than everyone could empty them!

"You won't be able to keep that up forever!" Queen Malice yelled nastily, laughing as Jasmine wobbled around with a heavy bucket in her hands.

"Oh dear," said King Merry as he carried another one to the side of Cloud Island. "My arms are getting very tired!"

"We have to keep going," Lolo said as she rushed over to help him empty the bucket over the edge of the cloud. "If the cotton candy gets any wetter, the island will break apart again and Queen Malice will have won."

Just then Jasmine peered up at Queen Malice's cloud and noticed something — it was moving upward. "Look!" she called.

As the girls watched, the cloud rose higher and higher.

Queen Malice came back into view as her thundercloud headed even higher. "Stop moving me!' she shrieked.

"It's not us!" Jasmine yelled up to her. "Your cloud's much lighter without all that rain, so it's floating away!"

As the thundercloud drifted farther, the rain slowed to a drizzle and then stopped.

"Nooooo!" Queen Malice wailed from far above.

"The new cloud's ready," called an imp from the cloud factory.

"Quick, empty the rest of the buckets," Lolo shouted. The girls rushed to pour the water onto the flowers below. Jasmine was going so fast that she accidentally let go of the bucket, and it fell over the side as well.

"Oops!" she said, peering over the edge. The bucket had landed upside down on the head of one of the Storm Sprites!

"Who turned out the lights?" he squawked, sticking his arms out and accidentally pushing another sprite off the flower and into a puddle of mud on the ground.

"Nice hat," Ellie called down to him.

"At least that washed the cotton candy off!" Jasmine laughed.

With the rain emptied, the girls went to help the imps, who were bringing basket after basket of new cloud over to the crack. Everyone helped smooth the cloud over the gap so that the cotton candy didn't show at all. Soon you couldn't even see where the rift had been.

Suddenly there was a loud cracking

sound. Ellie looked over at the violet pool just in time to see the ugly black thunderbolt shattering into hundreds of pieces.

"We've broken the spell!" she said delightedly.

Suddenly a screechy voice called from high above. "Nooooo!" Queen Malice yelled. "My beautiful thunderbolt!"

Her cloud was so high they could hardly see it anymore, but they could still hear Queen Malice's voice as she shouted nastily. "There are still three more of my thunderbolts in the kingdom and you'll never find them! I'll make sure that everyone is miserable! I'll make the fairies cry! I'll spoil the mermaids' fun! I will not be defeated. . . ."

Queen Malice's voice finally faded into the distance, and she and her gloomy cloud were gone.

"She's so mean!" Summer said, shivering a bit. She couldn't help feeling a little bit afraid of Queen Malice. She was so nasty. You never knew what she was going to do next, or when she would turn up.

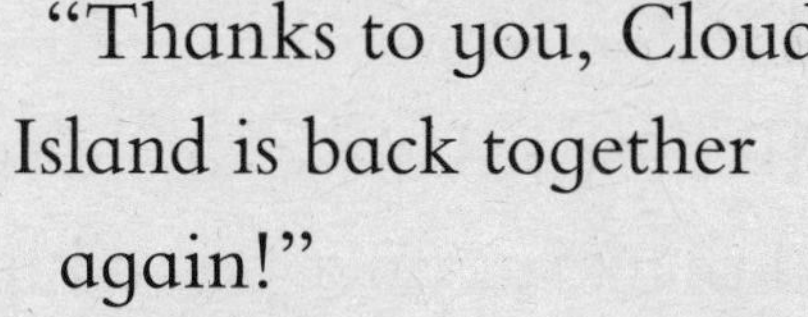

Lolo came over, smiling happily. "Thanks to you, Cloud Island is back together again!"

"Hooray!" the girls all cheered.

"I guess that means it's time for us to go home," Ellie sighed.

"Oh, but you'll come and visit us again, won't

you?" asked Lolo as all the weather imps gathered around to say good-bye. "We could never have fixed Cloud Island without you."

"We'd love to," said Jasmine.

"I think Cotton's saying good-bye as well," Summer said as the cloud bunny hopped over to her feet. She picked him up and stroked his tiny ears, trying not to feel sad.

All the girls gave the little rabbit a hug, and then Summer passed him to Lolo.

"Look up into the sky from your homes in the Other Realm," Lolo told them, "and you'll see animal shapes in the clouds. That's how you'll know that we're thinking of you."

"I'm sure you'll be back here soon," Trixi said grimly. "We know that Queen Malice hid six thunderbolts, and so far we've only found three of them."

"Wait a second!" Lolo cried. "We can't let you go without giving you a thank-you gift." She held up a beautiful, sparkling jewel. "This is a weather crystal," she said, handing it to Jasmine. "It gives you the power to change the weather for a little while."

Jasmine took the gleaming crystal. It had a golden glow and shimmered in the sunlight.

"Concentrate on the weather you want," Lolo told her.

Jasmine gazed at the crystal and thought hard. Suddenly glorious sunshine filled the sky!

"Oh, thank you!" Jasmine said, holding up the crystal for Summer and Ellie to see.

"Thank you so much," Ellie told Lolo.

"It's so beautiful!" said Summer, laughing as she danced in and out of the sunbeams.

"Ready to go, girls?" asked Trixi.

"Ready," they all said, holding hands and waiting for the whirlwind to carry them back home.

Trixi said the magic spell and tapped her ring. Silver stars shimmered all over them as the whirlwind started to form. It grew bigger and bigger, scooping them up and carrying them with it. Then there was a flash and they were back in Jasmine's bedroom again.

Ellie looked at the clock, but no time had passed. Somehow, time always stood still when they went to the Secret Kingdom.

"We'd better put these magical gifts away safely," said Summer, taking the unicorn horn out of her pocket and walking over to the Magic Box. The mirror started glowing and the lid magically opened. Summer placed the horn in one of the compartments, next to the magic map. Jasmine held up the weather crystal and they all looked at it one more time before she carefully placed it in the Magic Box. Three of the little

wooden compartments were filled now — and Jasmine could only imagine what exciting adventures they'd have before the little box was full.

"I guess we'd better get started with our homework," Ellie sighed.

"That's it!" Summer cried. "I know what you can write your story about — Cloud Island and the weather imps!"

"No one would believe me," said Ellie.

"Well, at least *we* know it's true!" Jasmine laughed.

Ellie grinned and opened her book happily. She couldn't wait to describe all the magical things she'd seen on Cloud Island — and imagine all the wonderful things they'd do on their next visit to the Secret Kingdom!

**In the next Secret Kingdom adventure, Ellie, Summer, and Jasmine visit**

# Mermaid Reef

**Read on for a sneak peek. . . .**

## A Message at School

"I'm starving!" Jasmine Smith cried as she joined her friends Ellie Macdonald and Summer Hammond at their usual table in the busy school cafeteria.

"We saved your space." Summer smiled. "Where have you been?"

"I left my headband in the classroom," Jasmine told her. Everyone had to wear the same navy-blue sweater, white top, and boring gray pants or skirt at school, but that didn't stop Jasmine from trying to brighten her uniform up a bit. She usually wore colorful barrettes or a pretty clip in her long dark hair. Today she was wearing a bright pink headband that matched her backpack.

As Jasmine pulled her lunchbox out of her bag, she noticed something else. Deep at the bottom of her backpack there was a familiar sparkly glow. . . .

"The Magic Box!" Jasmine whispered.

"What?" Ellie gasped, almost knocking her drink over in excitement. The Magic Box had never sent them a message at school before!

The box looked just like a beautiful wooden jewelry box. It had a curved lid and a mirror surrounded by six shiny jewels. Its sides were covered with carvings of fairies and other magical creatures. The three friends took turns looking after it, but it really belonged to King Merry, the ruler of a wonderful place called the Secret Kingdom.

The Secret Kingdom was a magical land full of unicorns, mermaids, pixies, and elves — but it had a terrible problem. When King Merry had been chosen by his subjects to rule the kingdom instead of his nasty sister, Queen Malice, the horrid queen had been so annoyed that she had thrown six enchanted thunderbolts into the most wonderful places in the land to ruin them and make everyone as miserable as she was.

King Merry had sent the Magic Box to find the only people who could help save the kingdom — Jasmine, Summer, and Ellie! The girls had already helped the king and his pixie assistant, Trixibelle, destroy three of the horrible thunderbolts. Now it looked like they were needed to find another one.

"We'll have to finish lunch when we come back," said Ellie as they rushed into the girls room. Time always stood still while they were in the Secret Kingdom, so no one would realize they were gone. But people might notice if they suddenly vanished in the middle of the cafeteria!

They closed the door of a stall and crowded around the box.

"The riddle's appearing!" Summer whispered.

They all watched eagerly as words started to form in the mirrored lid:

*"Another thunderbolt is near,*
*Way down deep in water clear.*
*Look on the bed that's in the sea,*
*Where more than fish swim happily!"*

Ellie slowly read out the rhyme. "What do you think that means?"

Jasmine frowned. "Well, the bottom of the sea is called the sea*bed* . . ."

Suddenly the Magic Box glowed again and the lid magically opened, revealing the six little wooden compartments inside. Three of the spaces were already filled with the wonderful gifts they'd been given by the people of the Secret Kingdom. There was a magical moving map that showed them all the places in the kingdom, a tiny silver unicorn horn that let them talk to animals, and a shimmering crystal that had the power to change the weather.

"Maybe the map will give us a clue," said Jasmine. She carefully took it out of the Magic Box and smoothed it flat. It showed the whole of the Secret Kingdom spread out beneath them, as if the girls were looking down at it from high above.

"Look," Jasmine said, pointing to the aquamarine sea. Waves were gently spilling onto the shore, colorful fish were playing in the water, and a beautiful girl was sitting on a rock, combing her hair.

As Ellie, Summer, and Jasmine watched, the girl dived off the rock into the sparkling water. Jasmine gasped as she saw that, instead of legs, the girl had a glittering tail!

"Did you see that?" she cried to the

others, who nodded excitedly. "She's a mermaid!"

Summer's eyes widened. "That must be it! 'More than fish swim happily' — we must be going to help mermaids!"

They leaned over the map again and watched the mermaid as she swam down to where an underwater town was marked. Ellie held the map up and looked at the place name. " 'Mermaid Reef,' " she read. "That must be where we're going."

Jasmine and Summer agreed, and the three girls quickly placed their fingertips on the jewels on the Magic Box.

Summer smiled at the others and said the answer to the riddle out loud:

"Mermaid Reef."

The green jewels sparkled and a glittering light beamed out from the mirror, throwing dancing patterns onto the walls. Then there was a golden flash and Trixi appeared, twirling in midair like a ballerina! Her blond hair was even messier than usual, but she had a huge grin and her blue eyes twinkled happily as she balanced on her leaf.

"Hi, Trixi," Ellie cried in delight as the pixie hovered gracefully just in front of the girls.

"Hello," Trixi said, smiling. "Goodness, where are we?"

"We're at school!" Jasmine told her.

"Oh," Trixi said as she flew around the bathroom stall on her little leaf. "This isn't at all what I thought an Other

Realm school would look like. Where do you all sit?"

The girls giggled. "We're not in a classroom," Summer explained. "This is just the bathroom. We had to make sure no one would see us being swept off to the Secret Kingdom."

"Of course, silly me." Trixi smiled, but then her face took on a worried expression. "Do you know where Queen Malice's next thunderbolt is?"

"We think so," Ellie told her. "It seems to be somewhere called Mermaid Reef."

"Then we must go at once!" Trixi exclaimed. "The mermaids will need our help."

"We *are* going to meet mermaids!" Summer squealed as she jumped up and down in excitement.

Trixi giggled, then tapped her ring and chanted:

*"The evil queen has trouble planned.*
*Brave helpers fly to save our land!"*

As she spoke those words, a magical whirlwind surrounded the girls, twisting and turning around them.

"Wheeee!" Summer shouted as the wind whipped her long blond hair around her face. "We're off on another adventure!"

Seconds later, the whirlwind put them down on a smooth green rock in the middle of the aquamarine sea. The girls were all delighted to be wearing their sparkly tiaras once again, although they were still in their school uniforms!

Jasmine looked around in surprise. "I thought we were going underwater?" she asked Trixi.

"We are!" Trixi said with a smile as she landed on the rock beside them, rolled up her flying leaf, and tucked it under her flower hat.

Suddenly the ground beneath them started to shake.

"What's going on?" Ellie cried.

The girls watched nervously as the water started to churn in front of them, foaming and frothing as something large and dark rose up out of the depths.

A huge green head appeared out of the water. Ellie and Jasmine gasped in fear and squeezed their eyes shut, but Summer broke out in a big grin. "Look!"

she cried, pointing at the beast's face. The creature blinked at them with sparkling brown eyes and gave them a lazy smile. "This isn't a rock we're standing on — it's the back of a gigantic sea turtle!"

"A lift from a friendly turtle is the only way to get to Mermaid Reef!" Trixi said, winking at the girls. The little pixie tapped her ring and a stream of purple bubbles shot out of it. The bubbles flew all around the girls in a whirlwhind, then burst over their heads, showering them with purple glitter.

"Hold on tight!" Trixi called, pointing to the top of the turtle's shell, where there was a ridge they could grab on to. "One . . . two . . ."

"Trixi, wait!" Jasmine cried. "We can't breathe underwater!"

But it was too late.

"Three!" Trixi called, tapping her ring once more, and with a great lurch the huge turtle dived deep into the sea. . . .

Read

# Mermaid Reef

to find out what
happens next!

Character Profile:
Jasmine
Smith

Family:
Jasmine lives with her mother and grandmother.
Favorite Color:
Pink
Loves:
Singing and dancing and being the center of attention!
Favorite Place in the Secret Kingdom:
The ice slides at Magic Mountain. Wheeeee!
Personality:
Fun and outgoing. If there's a problem, Jasmine will march in and sort things out!

# Favorite Places

From Cloud Island, Jasmine, Ellie, and Summer can look down over the whole of the Secret Kingdom. Far below them are all kinds of magical places. But where in the Secret Kingdom should you visit? Take our quiz to find out!

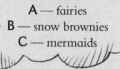

## Would you prefer to . . . ?

A — go to a beautiful beach
B — whiz down ice slides
C — swim underwater

## What type of Secret Kingdom creatures would you like to meet?

A — fairies
B — snow brownies
C — mermaids

## What kind of weather do you like?

A — sunshine
B — freezing cold, with lots of pink snow
C — wet

## What's your favorite activity?

A — building sand castles
B — ice-skating
C — singing in front of an audience

## Which gift would you most like to receive?

A — a garland of beautiful flowers
B — a pair of warm mittens
C — a pretty pearl necklace

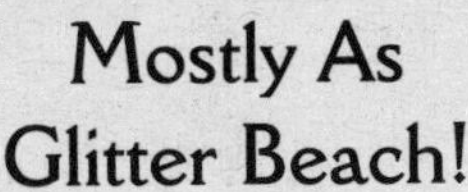

## Mostly As
## Glitter Beach!

You should go to Glitter Beach, where you can swim in the aquamarine sea, lie on the golden sand, and go to all the pretty fairy shops. Have fun!

## Mostly Bs
## Magic Mountain!

You should go to Magic Mountain, where snow brownies have lots of fun in the snow. You can slide down huge ice slides. Don't forget your cold-weather clothes!

## Mostly Cs
## Mermaid Reef!

You should go to Mermaid Reef and swim with Lady Merlana and the mermaids down in Coral City. If you're lucky, they might even sing for you!

# Which Magical Fairies Have You Met?

- ❑ The Rainbow Fairies
- ❑ The Weather Fairies
- ❑ The Jewel Fairies
- ❑ The Pet Fairies
- ❑ The Dance Fairies
- ❑ The Music Fairies
- ❑ The Sports Fairies
- ❑ The Party Fairies
- ❑ The Ocean Fairies
- ❑ The Night Fairies
- ❑ The Magical Animal Fairies
- ❑ The Princess Fairies
- ❑ The Superstar Fairies
- ❑ The Fashion Fairies
- ❑ The Sugar & Spice Fairies

RMFAIRY9